ΛΙΥ

ALBERT
THE ALBATROSS

Story and pictures by **SYD HOFF**

HarperCollins*Publishers*

Books by Syd Hoff

MY AUNT ROSIE

SYD HOFF'S ANIMAL JOKE BOOK

WHEN WILL IT SNOW?

WHERE'S PRANCER?

I Can Read Books®

BARKLEY

BARNEY'S HORSE

CHESTER

DANNY AND THE DINOSAUR

GRIZZWOLD ·

THE HORSE IN HARRY'S ROOM

JULIUS

LITTLE CHIEF

MRS. BRICE'S MICE

OLIVER

SAMMY THE SEAL

SANTA'S MOOSE

THUNDERHOOF

WHO WILL BE MY FRIENDS?

HarperCollins®, ⬛®, and I Can Read Book®
are trademarks of HarperCollins Publishers Inc.

ALBERT THE ALBATROSS
Copyright © 1961 by Syd Hoff
Copyright renewed 1989 by Syd Hoff
Printed in the United States of America.
All rights in this book are reserved.
Library of Congress Catalog Card Number: 61-5767
ISBN 0-06-022446-0 (lib. bdg.)

ALBERT
THE ALBATROSS

Albert was a bird.

He lived on the ocean.

He was an albatross.

Sailors liked to see him.

An albatross is good luck.

They were happy

when Albert followed their ship.

One day there was a storm.

The wind blew and blew and blew.

The sailors could not see Albert.

Albert could not see the sailors.

All he could see was the land.

"Have you seen the ocean?"

Albert asked a bird in a cage.

12

The bird was a parrot.

"Polly wants a cracker," said the bird.

"Have you seen the ocean?"

Albert asked a bird in a clock.

The bird was a cuckoo.

"Cuckoo-cuckoo," said the bird.

"Have you seen the ocean?"

Albert asked a bird in a tree.

The bird was a woodpecker.

"Tap-tap-tap," said the bird.

17

"Have you seen the ocean?"

Albert asked a bird on a church.

18

The bird was made of tin.

It could not say anything.

Albert flew into a store.

"I want this one for my trip,"

said a lady.

21

"What a pretty hat," said her friends.

"That bird looks real."

"Thank you," said the lady.

"I will wear it on the ship."

The people got on the ship.

Everyone waved good-by.

"Good-by," said the lady.

It was time for dinner.

"I know you!" said the captain.

"No, you don't," said the lady.

"Not you," said the captain.

"I know the bird on your hat."

"Oh!" said the lady.

"I don't want a real bird on my hat."

28

"We want a real bird," said the sailors.

"We want that albatross.

He is good luck."

"It is good luck that I found you,"

said Albert.

"Welcome home, Albert!" said everyone.

The End